NORA & NEIL

Coincidentally?

Coincidence or Fate?

NIDA ALI

To everyone struggling and fighting battles alone without giving up, you're doing great.

Prologue

I have always wondered how some people move through life with lightness in their steps, as if love never failed them, as if home were always a safe place. I used to envy them—those with easy laughter, soft eyes, and hearts untouched by betrayal.

I didn't grow up that way. My home was never warm or a safe place for me. It wasn't cruel to live in, but it was mostly cold. The silence, the distance, and the feeling of being unwanted, even when surrounded by people who were supposed to love.

They say family is everything, but what if your family is where the breaking began?

I learned at an early age that not all parents were perfect, and not all parents knew how to love. Some were too wounded to care, too tired to try, too absorbed in their chaotic life to notice the quiet suffering of their child. And with this, I became invisible. I stopped waiting for someone to care for me. I started building walls long before I knew what boundaries were. It wasn't about rebellion— it was about survival.

I was the child who never cried too loud, who never asked for more than what was given, who always carried the disappointment inside, and as I grew, I took the same version of myself into the world— quiet, reserved, careful. I let people see only what I wanted them to, never letting them know me. Because knowing me meant seeing the pain, and I wasn't sure anyone would stay if they did.

I think the hardest part of growing up is realizing that your parents are just ordinary people; flawed, afraid, sometimes selfish. But even then, it doesn't take away all the damage. It doesn't quiet the voice in your head that asks, *"Why wasn't I enough?"* It stays and it shapes you for the better. People who go through childhood trauma either become a better version of themselves or ruin their lives, there's no in between.

I am trying to learn to go easy on myself, to speak to the little girl inside me with kindness, to stop punishing her for needing love. I am learning that being soft is not the same as being weak. That feeling deeply is not something to be ashamed of.

And maybe—just maybe—life isn't about having a perfect beginning. Maybe it's about how to clear the mess, how you organize everything during chaos, how you handle the heartache, the empty spaces left behind by people who will not matter in your life a few years later, yet leave a mark forever.

This is not a story of blame.

It's a story of becoming.

Becoming the best version of yourself when things have never been better in life.

Part One
Nora

1

I was sitting in my usual spot, the right farther corner table at 'The Brewing Street Café', from where I could get a good view of the outside through the glass window. I observed everyone passing through the street while sipping my whipped iced latte, wondering what each of them had in their minds. Life seems to parade past me in a steady stream of motion. Everyone has a story behind their smiling faces. Most of us successfully hide our dreadful stories and keep moving along with time; some people don't.

We all have our very own limit of dealing with things and once we can't take it anymore, we explode in different ways—some people drown themselves in the ocean of work, some people give up everything and find solace in staying in their comfort zone and sleep for long hours together, and then some people keep fighting. At first, they fight to sleep and then they fight to get up from the bed, they fight to go to work, and engage themselves in social activities. They fight their appetite; they fight their will to do anything, and they mostly fight their tears that are ready to roll down any moment.

I watched the world unfold with keen eyes, noting everything and everyone. I could see a lot of people stuck to their phones while a few stared at their watches and frowned. Few faces were smiling, few seemed exhausted. I pondered for a while, trying to read the faces and their expressions- *what could they be thinking or what could they be going through at the moment in their lives?* I saw a half-bald man with fuming eyes; he seemed to have been in a fight with his wife and stormed out during the argument. There was a boy in a high school football uniform who seemed to have a crush on his friend walking along with him- his eyes were filled with love.

A man was pretending to read a newspaper, but he was actually checking out every woman who walked past him—lustful eyes, a woman with a baby then stopped in front of the café, she was tearing up and seemed lost but didn't lose the grip of her baby even when she was about to trip.

An old man, in his eighties, moved at a slower pace using his cane as if his life were dependent on it. He stopped for a while, turned his head slowly watching a group of college students rushing past him, laughing and giggling, running and being playful, his eyes blink and the fine lines on his forehead shows how much he was envious of these youngsters or I can say he yearns for his youth to return for once. I am sure he would give anything to get back to those good old days when he was in good health and sound mind.

I opened my diary and started to write.

21 August 2022

Sunday

11:30 am

Lost my youth to responsibilities.

No, I ain't complaining.

I wish that I'd enjoy,

Every moment that simply seems to pass by.

Losing hope and watching time fly,

I understand nothing, how and why?

I took a deep sigh and looked out of the window again.

I find peace in writing whatever I have in mind. It allows me to express my feelings without hesitation. I enjoy the process, it is more than an activity to me, it is a part of who I am. It gives me a feeling that I am talking to someone close, that there is someone who I can trust blindly, and I will never be embarrassed to share my vulnerable moments with. Most importantly, it will never judge me or get bored and leave me.

I continued to write.

I don't exist for most of the people around me. I have always lived this way, hiding myself from everyone, and now no one notices my presence anymore. The worst part is—it feels like nobody would ever miss me or even talk about me when I'm gone someday. It's all lies when people say they only need love to live a happy life and nothing else really matters. I hate attachments. It turns you into someone weak. I have seen how attachments can lead to pain, how people leave or change, and I am not ready to put myself up for that kind of hurt once again. So, I keep my distance, pushing people away just enough to feel safe. You become a puppet of your feelings. You wait, you cry, you smile. and you do all sorts of stupid things that you've never done before. I think it is best not to fall into this hopeless yet beautiful trap. But...

I stopped writing for a moment as I was quite embarrassed to continue further, but this was the only thing I could do to speak for myself, so I started writing again.

I have been lying to myself all this time because I'm afraid to admit the truth. Yes, the truth that only I know, and I've never dared to tell this to anyone because I hate to feel feeble. It is also my biggest fear, and the truth is that I desperately want to be loved. I still find myself longing for someone to hold on to me, to prove that love doesn't always have to end in loss. I, too, need someone to love me, care for me, smile at me, walk with me, and feel for me. I crave the warmth of connection, the feeling of being understood, but the thought of depending on someone scares me. I have always told people that I don't care about such things but the truth is that I am a hopeless romantic and I dream of a beautiful life with the one who is just right for me but again I am afraid to get attached to someone and get my heart broken as I have already been through this and I am done once and for all. I don't think that I can afford getting attached to someone to the extent where I am the only one hurting. I lack the courage, and there are several reasons behind this.

I closed the diary and walked back to my apartment.

2

I pushed open the glass doors of Snow Moon Solutions, the office building, as the cool blast of air-conditioning greeted me like an old friend. Another Monday, another week of juggling deadlines and expectations. I smiled politely at the receptionist, waved to the security guard who always gave me a thumbs-up, and stepped into the elevator. Floor 11. Marketing and Communications.

As the elevator doors slid open, I was instantly welcomed by the faint hum of conversations, ringing phones, and the clatter of keyboards. I walked past the open workspace, where familiar faces greeted me with tired grins or slight nods. It was a culture of silent support— everyone drowning, but waving anyway.

"Morning, Nora!" chirped Rhea, the overly enthusiastic intern who had joined just two weeks ago.

"Morning, Rhea. You're in early." I replied, forcing a smile.

"Wanted to get ahead on the campaign data analysis. Mr. Griffin gave me some extra work." She said cheerfully. I blinked. Poor thing didn't realize yet that "extra work" was Mr. Griffin's love language.

I reached my cubicle, a modest space with a pinboard of motivational quotes, my calendar scribbled with deadlines, and a tiny plant that was somehow still alive. My desk was already stacked with files I hadn't asked for.

Before I could even sit, my phone buzzed. A message from Sam:

"Boss wants to see you. Now."

I groaned inwardly and walked toward the glass-walled corner cabin, Mr. Griffin's office.

Mr. Griffin, the man behind most people's migraines, sat behind his desk, eyes glued to his laptop screen. He didn't look up when I entered.

"You're late." He said without emotion.

"It's 9:05, Mr. Griffin."

"Five minutes late is still late."

I didn't respond. I had learned to let the jabs slide off my skin like water on glass. Reacting only fed his power.

"I need the preliminary draft of the GoGreen project pitch by tomorrow. Not Thursday. I want the creatives reviewed, the presentation deck done, and the copy polished." He said, still typing.

"Mr. Griffin, that's not possible. We need the graphics team to finish their part of work first, and we haven't received approval for the budget yet."

"Make it possible, Miss Jones." His voice was cold steel. *"You're a senior executive, not a college student asking for deadline extensions."*

I nodded, jaw clenched. *"I'll do my best."*

"Not best. I want results."

As I left his office, I exhaled deeply. How could someone be so constantly unreasonable and yet so... confident in their tyranny?

Back at my desk, I opened my planner and mentally restructured my entire day. So much for lunch breaks or breathing space. I picked up my phone and messaged my team:

"Team huddle in 10 mins. Conference Room B."

Ten minutes later, I stood in front of the team—tiny but mighty tribe.

There was Phil, late thirties, grumpy by default, but an organizational wizard. He had a sarcastic comment for everything, and yet, he was the first to stay late when a teammate was drowning.

Next was Anna, the social media strategist. A firecracker in heels, always scrolling through trends, sipping on bubble tea, and swearing she would quit 'any day now.'

Ethan, the quiet designer, barely spoke but somehow turned vague ideas into visual magic. His headphones were practically glued to his ears, and no one knew what music he listened to— but it worked.

And finally, Rhea, the intern, all enthusiasm and spreadsheets.

"Okay, listen up." I began rubbing my temples. *"We've just been voluntold by Mr. Griffin to submit the GoGreen pitch tomorrow. That includes the entire deck— copy, creatives, campaign outline, and everything."*

Anna's eyes widened. *"Tomorrow? Is he high?"*

Ethan raised an eyebrow but said nothing.

"I know it's unfair," I admitted. *"But we're in survival mode. We do this, we buy ourselves breathing room."*

Phil snorted. *"Until he decides he wants a new version the next day."*

"True," I said with a sigh. *"But let's just get through this first. Rhea, I'll need you to chase down the budget numbers and competitor data. Phil, help me build the deck skeleton and align timelines. Anna, rough ideas for the social media rollout. Ethan, I know the creatives were supposed to take three days, but can you get me a draft by tonight?"*

Ethan simply nodded.

"We're pulling a late one, guys. I'll get dinner delivered. Just... bear with me."

As the team dispersed, grumbling but determined, I sat back in my chair and looked around the office.

Despite the chaos, despite Mr. Griffin's impossible expectations, this place-these people-had become something like a second home. Dysfunctional, noisy, tiring... but familiar.

✳✳✳

The office lights were dimmed, but the marketing corner still glowed from screens and scattered lamps. Half-eaten pizza boxes were stacked at the side table, and the whiteboard was filled with post-its and rough scribbles.

I stretched; my back was aching. The pitch deck was finally coming together. Phil had rewritten the timeline thrice, Anna had created a hashtag campaign that actually made them laugh, and Ethan's visuals were yet again—stunning.

"Guys, you're amazing," I said softly.

Anna gave me a thumbs-up, chewing on cold garlic bread. *"We know."*

"I can't believe we're doing this for a man who thinks 'deadline' means 'make it painful,' ugh," Phil muttered.

They laughed. Even Ethan cracked a smile.

As the clock crept past 10:45 pm, I glanced at my team-tired, overworked, but still pushing forward.

And then, I thought of Mr. Griffin, of all the pressures, the unacknowledged victories, the stress migraines, and skipped meals. But I also thought of these nights-the ones that tested their limits but reminded me why I kept showing up.

Because even in a broken system, you could find moments of unity. Even under pressure, you could find strength in the people around you.

And that, I realized, was enough for now.

3

I got off work at 11:30 pm and was headed to get a cab, just when I heard someone calling me out—

"Nora, NORA!" As I turned back to follow the voice, I found us standing face to face. It was my only friend since middle school.

"Hey, Violet."

"Wow! So, am I finally visible to you? Where have you been yesterday? I called you several times to go out for dinner, and you ignored my calls. Would you like to explain that to me, please?"

"Well, you see, I was at the library," I replied.

*"Yeah, right. The library. Your safe place, or should I call it **your escape place**."* She looked at me angrily, and I chuckled.

"I think you need something cold down your throat to calm down. How about an iced latte?"

"You really know how to change my mind, and I can't decline your sweet offer."

We both enjoyed chatting about how things were going in our lives. Just her presence cheered me up. Violet and I have been friends since middle school. I was always an introvert who was sometimes called a nerd, and I did not have any social skills. So to sum up, I did not have any friends, but then there was her who was always there for me and even fought with others when anyone mocked me in school. We even went to the same college, but it broke our hearts when I had to move to Edinburgh a few years ago. She was the only one who never judged me.

She was there whenever I needed a shoulder to cry on, without asking me what happened until I told her everything. Isn't it just wonderful to have someone by your side who you can rely on, without any expectations. We have been inseparable since then. She followed me to Edinburgh six months ago and moved in with me temporarily until her company apartment was ready. She spent a month with me and then moved to her company's apartment. It's a bit far away from my place, so she promised to meet me every weekend. We grabbed some doughnuts before parting ways.

***

It felt a little lonely after Violet had gone. I have been used to living a lonely life, but when she was here, it felt less lonely, and now, I was all alone once again. I dropped on the couch with the TV remote in hand thinking to watch a movie but the moment I turned it on there was a show about happy families, I switched the channel and there was a movie scene with a family of three; parents with their seven-year-old daughter having fun at the amusement park, laughing, and eating candy. I turned off the TV and stared at the blank screen, watching my reflection on it, sitting alone, in an empty house.

I recollected the time when Violet and I tried to cook dinner for the first time. We were in high school; her parents were away on a two-day vacation to the beach. God, that was a terrible idea.

I stood in the kitchen with my hands on my hips, staring at the chaos on the counter like I was about to wage war. Flour, eggs, tomatoes, pasta... and— wait, was that a half-eaten chocolate bar?

"Violet, why is there chocolate in the vegetable basket?" I asked, raising an eyebrow.

Perched lazily on a stool with a whisk in one hand and a cucumber slice in the other, she replied without missing a beat, "Emergency backup snack. You never know when dinner might turn into a disaster."

I rolled my eyes. "It's dinner. We're making pasta. How hard can it be?"

"Famous last words." She muttered, popping the cucumber into her mouth like some kind of wise old sage.

The plan was simple: girls' night in, just me and Violet, cooking dinner and catching up. Execution, though? Already heading south. We followed the recipe.

Step 1: Boil water.

Easy. Child's play.

I turned on the stove and set a pot of water on it. "See? Simple."

Ten seconds later, Violet was beside me, peering dramatically into the pot.

"It's not boiling."

"It just got on the stove, Violet."

"I'm just saying. This is how it starts. You wait too long for water to boil, and next thing you know, you're 30, single, and still waiting."

"You're 18."

"I rounded off just for fun. Doesn't matter, focus on the word 'single' for now."

I chuckled and moved on to chopping onions. I peeled one and started slicing when Violet gasped behind me.

"You're not wearing goggles?! Rookie mistake!"

Before I could answer, she vanished down the hall and returned looking like a kitchen ninja—neon pink swimming goggles and a bright blue bandana.

I blinked. "You look like you're about to swim a relay and rob the pantry."

"Function over fashion." She said, striking a pose and attacking tomatoes with the focus of a samurai. "Also, I've watched MasterChef. They cry less than we do because they come prepared."

"Pretty sure they cry because Gordon Ramsay yells at them."

"You yell at me when I steal your fries. Same thing."

I snorted, accidentally flinging a slice of onion across the counter.

"See? It's already starting." She said ominously. "The chaos is rising."

"Don't jinx it, girl," I shouted.

I reached for the garlic, just as Violet pointed at the pot.

"Uh… is the pot supposed to do that?"

I glanced over. "That's just the stove, relax."

But then the pot began to shake slightly.

"...Did you remember to put only water in it?" Violet asked, eyes narrowing.

"Yes! And a little salt!"

"How much salt?"

I hesitated. "I might've... eyeballed it."

She stared at me like I'd just committed a crime. "Girl, that pot's got more salt than your dating life."

I gasped, hand on my chest. "Wow. The betrayal. In my own home."

Just then, the pot let out a loud pop, and we both jumped.

"I think it's mad," Violet whispered.

"It's boiling. That's good."

"Boiling? It sounds like it's plotting our demise."

Meanwhile, my onions were turning a little too golden. I turned around and— yep. They were officially crispy.

"Uh, Nora? Your onions look... toasty."

I rushed over and scraped them off the pan. "Okay, okay! Just a little crunchy. Adds texture."

"They're basically onion chips now."

We both burst into laughter. Wiping my eyes, I tried to refocus. "Okay. Pasta. Let's do this."

I grabbed the spaghetti and dumped half the pack into the pot.

"Wait!" Violet cried. "Aren't we supposed to break it first?"

"Break it? Who breaks spaghetti?"

"My aunt does. Says it fits the pot better."

"That's criminal."

"That's practical!"

While we bickered, the ends of the spaghetti stuck out of the pot like rebellious little antennae. I tried to push them in, but they snapped.

Time for the tomato sauce.

"Okay, blend the tomatoes," I said, handing her the blender.

She tossed the tomatoes in, added garlic, and looked around. "Where's the lid?"

"Uh... not sure. Just hold your hand on it?"

"You sure?"

"No. But we're brave."

Mistake number two.

The blender roared-and tomato sprayed everywhere. The ceiling, the cabinets, our shirts. We froze, drenched in red.

I shut it off. "Okay, maybe that was a really bad idea."

We stood there in stunned silence, dripping.

"We look like extras from a zombie movie." She said.

And then we lost it. I was laughing so hard I had to lean on the fridge.

Violet wiped sauce from her cheek. "Should we just order pizza?"

"Yes." I gasped, still wheezing.

We collapsed onto the couch-tired, messy, and laughing like maniacs. I grabbed my phone and called our favorite pizza place.

"Next time," Violet said, "we cook something easier. Like toast."

"Even that's risky in our hands," I muttered.

As we waited for pizza to arrive, surrounded by a kitchen that looked like a war zone, Violet glanced at me with a grin.

"Well, we may not be chefs, but we make one hell of a mess."

"And great memories," I said with a smile.

We raised our soda cans in a mock toast.

"To the disaster duo."

"To pasta disasters and pizza salvation."

I smiled thinking of that time when we could've burned down the apartment, and then when I looked around, it was just me. Lying in my bed, staring at the ceiling, full of restlessness due to overflowing thoughts. I hated these fake happy families. No family is perfect. I know what happens behind closed doors. You become family when you are close to someone who knows you well, who understands you, and loves you with all your imperfections. I kept switching sides all night, and then I could see the sun rays chasing away the darkness and lighting the sky slowly and peacefully.

3

Yet another Sunday, and I was here again, at 'The Brewing Street Café'.

"Hey! Morning, Nora. So, it's your usual order again?"

"Morning, Alex. Yes, please."

Alex has been working here for over a year. He is young and enthusiastic. We got to know each other as I came here every Sunday morning. At first, I was being myself, completely reserved, but Alex has a friendly disposition and has the talent to make friends quickly.

I was waiting for my coffee at the counter when Violet called and asked me to join her for shopping. I was on the call, picked up my coffee, and started walking toward my table. I was so into the conversation that I did not see someone coming from the other side and stopping right in front of me. I was startled, and my coffee almost spilled. I heard a soft yet deep voice.

"You forgot this."

My eyes were still fixated on his white sneakers. I slowly moved my head up to look at his face. Light blue baggy jeans matched with a loose white shirt tucked a little on one side. His hair was messy yet seemed perfectly done, and his deep-set hazel eyes. I saw his pupils dilating when I looked into his eyes. He was holding my diary in his hand.

"You forgot your diary at the counter." He said, trying to sneak a look, rummaging through the pages. I immediately snatched my diary from his hand.

"Reading someone's diary is disrespectful," I said in a frustrated tone.

"Oh, I am really sorry. I didn't mean to." His voice was still soft.

I started to walk away from him.

"Hey, not thanking people when they help you is disrespectful." This time, he sounded annoying to me. I don't like it when guys try to act smart and funny around me. He immediately had his first strike on my list of 'Things that I hate'. I ignored him and went to my seat. I was still holding my phone close to my ears and could hear Violet babbling about shopping. I told her that I would call her back.

He was sitting at a table across from my table on my left side, and when I accidentally glanced at him, he smirked at me and sipped his coffee proudly.

He looks cute but has an annoying personality. I thought to myself and looked away. I left after a while to meet Violet. We were holding a dozen bags when we went back to her apartment. We had a grilled cheese chicken sandwich to fill our empty stomachs, and then I returned to my apartment. I was so exhausted that I didn't know how quickly I fell asleep.

4

This week has been exhausting for me, too much work. I was feeling suffocated, so I thought to take a walk outside to get some fresh air. I was in my pyjamas, my hair was a complete mess, so I just made a pony, roughly with my hands, slipped into my flip flops, and went out. As I strolled for some time, I encountered a familiar face staring at me from across the street. The moment our eyes met, he smirked, and I quickly recognized him. He started walking toward me, and I was getting anxious.

"What are you doing here? Are you stalking me? How did you know I live here? What are you trying to do?" I fired him with questions.

"Woah, relax. I am not a stalker, okay? And I definitely do not have any ulterior motives. Just look at yourself. You look like a mess. What makes you think I am stalking you?" He looked at me from head to toe.

"I didn't know you lived here, and for your information, I live in this apartment, too." I was totally embarrassed after hearing his defense. I couldn't utter another word. *"What's the problem with you? Why do you think that everything is only about you? If you have got some time to spare, then look around you, there's a lot going on here."*

My mind was blown the moment I heard him spill those words. It wasn't actually his words that triggered me, but it was 'me' and 'my thoughts'. I was already feeling down, and his words, which in reality had nothing to do with me, hit me hard at that time. A tear rolled down my face slowly, and my eyes were burning with rage.

"What the hell is YOUR problem? Why are you trying to act like you know me when you don't? Who do you think you are to judge me? Do you think that you can easily get away with your say? You are no one to look down on me. You have no right to do that, do you hear me?"

I found myself yelling at him, and then I rushed back to my apartment. I sat leaning against my bed on the floor with my arms folded around my knees. I tried my best not to recall those hurtful memories, but it seemed like someone had knocked down the door that I had locked to keep myself away from. One by one, tears dropped, and shortly after, I was sobbing.

I have tried my best to get rid of this feeling, but it seems to be haunting me, chasing me all the time, and I have nowhere to run away from this. I have lived my whole life being a 'nobody', and whenever I wanted to do something for myself, I was called 'selfish'; whenever I stood up for myself, I was told that I was difficult to talk to and that I was full of myself. I have seen all sorts of things in life. From my parents getting into ugly fights, my father leaving the dinner table, smashing a porcelain, and walking out slamming the door behind, to my mother weeping every day.

They were always so busy hurting each other that they completely forgot about me. They never realized that I had to see them fight every day, and I was just a scared little kid. It was way worse when I heard my mother scream and the loud noise of things breaking and smashing in the background. I used to hide myself under the table in my room with my eyes tightly closed and both hands pressing my ears. I would cry until things calmed down. I couldn't help the situation then.

As I grew up, I cursed myself and still can't get rid of the guilt that I could do nothing at all to help them or make them understand how terribly it all affected me. I never went to school picnics. It was a way to punish myself, thinking that my parents were having a hard time, and if they were not happy, then I didn't deserve to be happy as well. I never had friends because there was no one who could understand what was going on inside this little head, but one day, Violet walked into the classroom. She had moved from another city as her father was a manager in a global company, and he was transferred to Preston. Violet broke all the walls that I had created, and she has been there for me since then, always.

Once I graduated from college, I wanted to move out and take up a job in another city, and that was the first time I was called selfish by my mother. I still don't get it, how was it my fault that things were rough between my parents. I cried silently every day and night, blaming myself for being born into this world. I prayed earnestly to die so that everything would be peaceful. A year later, I moved to Edinburgh and started working as an intern in a small publishing firm. I started reading books when I was nine. It was a way for me to escape reality and dive deep into the world of imagination. I love to see books stacked in the shelves. It gives me an adrenaline rush just to be near books. I met a guy who was also an intern there, Luke. After spending a month there, I realized that he had a crush on me.

There were clear signals that he liked me, and one day he asked me out. I was new to this feeling, but I liked everything he did for me. He had good convincing skills, and I couldn't say 'no' to anything he asked me for.

We dated for about five months, and I fell in love with his humble nature. I was so blinded by this feeling that I could see nothing else, but everything started to fall into place when one day he asked me to quit my job. The publishing firm had decided to continue with only one intern and make them a full-time permanent employee.

That jerk had the audacity to come to me and ask me to give up my efforts for him. When I resisted and told him that this job was very important to me as well and that we should leave this decision to the firm, he called me 'selfish'. He was well aware that the firm would choose me over him, and he could not take it. My mind didn't respond for a while to him calling me 'selfish' like what I had ever done to be labelled as a self-centered person. He was the one to get the permanent position, and I came to know the reason why he was chosen over me later.

Now, I understand that everything was my fault. My life, my struggles, my relationships, everything. I have always given a lot to everyone without expecting anything in return, and this was my biggest mistake in life. This world doesn't work that way. I always put others before myself. Being overly empathetic can lead you to ruin your peace of mind.

5

I was still lying on the cold floor, crumpled, when I woke up. It was a Sunday, but I decided not to go out. After freshening up, I went to the balcony to absorb some sunlight to energize myself. I looked at the sky, and it gave me a serene feeling. I took a long, deep breath, trying to inhale a lot of fresh air, but the next moment I was startled when I looked down. I saw that annoying face outside our building. He was coming from his morning walk, it seems.

I don't know what happened, but I immediately ran to the drawing room, dropped myself onto the couch, and closed my eyes. A moment later, I asked myself what I was doing and why I was even hiding myself from him. I didn't do anything wrong, but I felt a little guilty after lashing out at him last night without knowing anything. I decided to apologize to him if we ever met again, which I would definitely love to avoid in this lifetime.

I spent the whole day at home. Cleaning and doing laundry consumed most of the time, and after doing all of the chores, I was so exhausted that I didn't have the strength to cook myself dinner. My tummy was growling, so I quickly ordered a pizza, which arrived within twenty minutes. I scrolled my phone watching some funny videos, meanwhile enjoying every bite of the pizza to fill my starving stomach.

***

So, it finally happened. It started raining suddenly when there had been no news in the weather report this morning. It was rush hour, I got off work and was looking for a cab. I stood under the shed of a toy store behind me and used my bag over my head to save myself from the rain to go back and forth trying to catch a ride. I saw a white car slowing down and stopping in front of me. The window glass moved down, and someone signaled me to get in. It was pouring so heavily that the face was blurry to me. It took me a while to recognize him.

"Hey, neighbor? Here!" He waved at me. *"This is your stalker."* He said loudly. *"Come, get in the car, I'll drop you. I am going home anyway."*

I looked around to make sure no one heard him. I hurried toward his car, he opened the door, and asked me to get in. I hesitated. I had no choice but to accept his offer. It was very awkward once I was inside his car. We both said nothing for a long time. I silently enjoyed the sound of the rain, looking outside, and it was ruined in another moment.

"So, where do you live again?" He asked with a serious face.

"What?" I responded angrily, and he burst into laughter.

"Yes, this is what I am talking about. I appreciate the passion in your expression when you're mad." I turned my head to look outside, sulking at his stupid talk. *"If I'm not wrong, you lack social skills."* He said dryly.

I chose not to answer.

"Are you okay?" This time, he sounded sincere. *"Well, you didn't come to the café yesterday."* I looked at him, and as I was about to speak, the car stopped.

"We're home. You go ahead. I need to run an errand quickly." I got out of the car and stood there watching him go. He put his head out from the window pane and waved, but this time he didn't seem annoying to me. It felt like I'd never seen him in a bright light, or maybe I was being judgmental and had already declared that he was guilty of the crime of being an annoying jerk.

6

I got back from work and received a call from Mom. *"I need a break from your dad."* She spoke. I had mixed feelings. A part of me was sad, but I was happy to see that finally my mother had gathered the courage to think about her happiness and live with a sense of freedom.

I recollected the night that was a nightmare for me while I was wide awake.

Our house was never a home, especially that evening. It was a war zone with floral curtains. I was fourteen and fragile in ways only I understood. I sat curled on the edge of my bed. The walls were thin. They had always been. But tonight was a little different. Tonight was uglier than the usual.

"You think I wanted this life?" Dad's voice roared from the living room. "You think I dreamed of coming home to this misery every day?"

I froze. I knew that those words weren't aimed at me, but they pierced just the same. I clutched the sleeves of my hoodie, pulling them over my palms, rocking slightly. My heart pounded badly as if it was trying to escape.

"Oh, don't act like you're the victim here." Mom's broken voice followed. "You've done nothing but blame me for everything for years. I sacrificed everything, and you—you just stomped all over it."

The next thing I heard was a crash; maybe a glass, maybe a vase. I couldn't tell anymore; I didn't want to. I wanted to disappear, escape all of this. I stood up and tiptoed across the floor, gently opening the bedroom door just an inch enough to see what was happening outside.

Dad was standing by the fireplace, his hands clenched into fists at his sides, his face red with fury. Mom stood across from him, trembling but defiant, eyes glassy with tears in them. Between them was the coffee table that had been knocked slightly off-center, a book lying face down on the carpet like it too had given up.

"I should've left the moment you started treating me like a furniture," Mom shouted in a cracked voice. "But—but I stayed for her."

I stiffened the moment I heard these words. So, I was the reason for this pain? This rage?

"Don't you dare throw that in my face." Dad snarled. "You think staying made things better? All you did was poison our relationship with your bitterness."

There was a complete silence for a while and then...

"I hate you sometimes," Mom whispered. The words were soft but landed like a blade.

I closed the door quietly and sank to the floor. The words that I had heard that night cut me deep down and left a wound that would never heal. My fingers trembled as I covered my ears. Their voices echoed inside my head all night, and it does till now. I wanted to cry, but the tears wouldn't come. A cold numbness settled in my chest. Heavy, permanent.

I didn't sleep a wink that night. I stared at the ceiling, and my mind raced with silent vows.

I would never fall in love.

I would never marry. And children? I couldn't imagine bringing a child into a world where love turned into war, where promises were used as weapons later, and where silence was a punishment.

No child deserved to grow up feeling like a collateral damage. I think all of this helped me grow with maturity and a sense of responsibility at an early age.

Years later, now, I still flinch at raised voices, still avoid loud arguments in public places. Happy couples made me skeptical. I knew what people didn't see. What love could turn into when time, resentment, and pain took over. I fell for Luke because he treated me with kindness, I fell into his trap because of his humble behaviour, and I was deceived yet again. When I met Luke, I forgot about my vows until he showed me his true colors.

I recalled all of it when...

"Hello? Nora?" Mom's voice over the phone brought me back to the present.

"Okay, so what next?" I asked her dryly. There was silence for a moment. I didn't know how to express what I was feeling. I have never been close to my parents, but I have always put myself into my mother's place and tried to imagine what it would be like to live such a life where your husband doesn't care about you at all, and you become the only target of all of his frustration. When your only child doesn't step up to help you in any way, showing a clear sign of cowardice.

"I don't know." She spoke after a pause.

"Well, then you can come over and live with me for as long as you want."

"Would that be okay with you?" She replied after much thought.

"Yes, of course. Why not?"

"Okay, I'll come to you this weekend."

I felt much better when she agreed to live with me. It meant that she wanted to bond with me, the bond that we never had, and the connection that I have always yearned for.

***

I was too occupied with my mom visiting me. I spent my weekends taking her to places she told me she'd like to visit. Violet often joined to enjoy food prepared by Mom, as she missed home-cooked meals a lot. This weekend, all three of us binged on shopping and then had dinner in a fancy restaurant. I wanted to show Mom all the finer places and give her an experience of everything that was within my limits. I've had no time to go to the library or the café, and when I realized it had already been a month since my mom came to Edinburgh. Time flies by when you are with your loved ones.

I called Dad a few times, but he never responded or called me back. I can understand what he must be feeling. Mom and I have both been trying to put aside the awkwardness and live comfortably. It was only silence for the first couple of days when mom came, but I'm getting used to it now, and actually, it feels great. The apartment now feels like home, it smells of homemade food when I come back home from work. It makes me feel much better coming back home and having someone waiting for me rather than coming back to an empty place.

I was at the café after a long time. The moment I entered, Alex looked at me and then looked at someone sitting at the left corner table.

"Hey, Neil. Look who's here." Alex waved at him.

"ALEX, what are you doing?" I mumbled.

"Hello, um-morning." Neil immediately looked at me, his eyes shined and he grinned nervously.

"Hi," I said awkwardly.

"We haven't seen you around in a while. Hope everything's okay with you?" Alex asked me curiously.

"We? Who else?" I enquired.

"Me!" Alex responded in a squeaky voice immediately.

"I mean, I haven't seen you around lately. That's what I meant, yeah." Alex answered nervously, correcting himself as if he had been caught in the act.

"Yeah, right. Well, my mom is visiting me, so I have been totally stuck with this and that. We are spending a lot of time together."

"Oh, I see. That's great to know. So, the coffee's on me today. How does that sound?"

"Perfect!" I gave Alex a thumbs up and waited for my coffee. I tried my best to avoid making eye contact with Neil. Most of the time, I was looking outside, but whenever I looked at him, I found him staring at me.

"Why is he acting so weird today?" I asked myself.

Although I had my diary with me but I couldn't focus on writing anything. I ran out of words due to lack of concentration, so I opened a random page from my diary and started reading something that I wrote ages ago.

It's You

The sunshine and the clear skies,

My wandering eyes met his eyes.

It felt like time stopped for a moment, and my heart skipped a beat,

I couldn't hear anything or feel the summer heat.

His smile filled my empty heart with happiness,

His mere presence took away all my loneliness.

When the day ended and it was time to say goodnight,

I waited for the next day to see him again, with every sleepless night.

Even if we can't be together,

I want these memories to last forever.

Nothing can be so good and true,

'Cause now I look at someone and you don't know that 'It's You!'.

I took a moment to feel it, and I don't know why, but I looked at Neil after reading this. My perspective of him was changing. At first, he seemed to me like a person I would never want to see in my life, but eventually things changed, and when I look at him now, I feel better. His mere presence assures me that someone is looking out for me. I can't get it; I don't know what or how things have changed, but now I know one thing which is for sure that I don't hate to see him around me anymore.

7

I was born in the city of Preston, Lancashire. My parents fell in love and got married at a young age, and then they had me. I think this was one of the reasons why our lives were twisted. I think about it every now and then- *Would things have been different if they had not been married and taken some time to understand each other first?* I always think that I may be the reason for making them fall out of love. If they had enjoyed their life spending some good time together, trying to feel each other, we would have been a 'happy family'. When my parents had me, their lives changed.

Dad started working hard to give us a better life, and my mom struggled all alone, taking care of me. Both of them were exhausted by the end of the day, which used to turn into frustration. Dad would come home tired, and Mom, who had suffered all day with the chores, cooking, cleaning, and taking care of an infant, expected him to become her comfort. Mom searched for heartfelt words and appreciation if there was no help from him, while Dad needed someone to sit with him and ask about his day. Their expectations grew with time, but no one wanted to put effort into this relationship.

They immersed themselves in their part of work, ignoring their feelings. There used to be complete silence as soon as Dad got home from work. No one spoke, and the moment Mom started talking, I could only hear them yelling at the top of their lungs. All I did was shudder in a corner and cry silently. So, when I entered my teenage, I began to avoid our 'eating dinner together' custom by either having my dinner before or after my parents did. By doing this, I was able to save myself from a lot of drama and hurt. I thought that distancing myself from them would be the best for all of us, but now, when I think about it, I know that I was wrong.

My mother was lonely. She had no one to talk to or share her feelings with, and my Dad, well, all fathers struggle living a lonely life while working hard for their family. I wish only if I could have been a good daughter to them, only if I could link their hearts, fill them with joy, and rekindle their love, only if... I still can't get myself out of the guilt that I never tried to understand my Dad's silent efforts, and I was never there for my mother. Only if they both had tried a little more, things might have been different. They would be less lonely, and I would be living differently, too.

My head was overwhelmed with all these thoughts, and I couldn't stop overthinking while I sat in the hospital waiting to hear from the doctor. Earlier this morning, I had received a call and they asked how I was related to Mrs. Emma Jones, as my number was found in her emergency contacts. I confirmed that I was her daughter and enquired what the phone call was regarding.

The call was from the hospital informing me that my mother had fallen down a flight of stairs in our apartment building and was severely injured. She was taken to the hospital after someone called the ambulance immediately, but she was bleeding profusely, and she was not responding. My feet and palms were cold when I heard the details, I collapsed on the chair behind me, and my legs were shivering. I tried to get up but couldn't move. I somehow composed myself in a few moments and quickly headed to the hospital. I called Violet on my way.

When I reached there, I saw that Mom was being moved to the ICU from the ER, and Neil was walking along with the staff. He was quite surprised to see me. I could see it in his eyes. He tried to calm me down so that I wouldn't panic and got me some water after helping me to sit in the waiting area. I called Dad about five times, and there was no response, so I left him a text informing him about the whole situation. It was just afternoon and the sun was still out. Neil sat beside me.

"Thanks," I said in a low, cracked voice.

"No problem. Everything will be fine. Don't worry, I am here with you." He slowly moved his palm on my shoulders, gently patting me. I looked into his eyes, and the tears that I've been holding back, trying to act strong, began to fall. I buried my face into my hands and cried like a baby; however, what surprised me more was that he was the first person to say something otherwise.

"It's okay, cry all you want. Don't keep it in, let it all out. It will make you feel better. You don't have to pretend to be strong all the time. You've gone through a lot, and tears are not a sign of weakness, so don't be bothered by what anyone thinks about you, just know that this is your life that you're living, and you have the right to live your life however you want." He embraced me as if he was ready to take away all my pain. It took me some time to steady myself. Neil got me a bottle of water and asked if I wanted to eat something, to which my answer was 'No'.

Violet came to the hospital after getting my call. After all, she was the one who's always been like a family to me. She looked at me and hugged me tightly. *"Mom will be fine; you don't stress yourself too much. I am here with you."* She then looked at Neil and asked, *"Anyways, who's this?"* I told her about Neil. *"I want to know everything about him later."* She demanded. She was with me all day, trying to comfort me and giving Neil a side eye every now and then.

The doctor told us that it would take some time for them to confirm her situation as she still has not regained consciousness. We both waited patiently. My phone rang, and it was Dad.

"Hello, Dad."

"What happened? How is Emma now? Send me the hospital's address. I am taking the first flight to Edinburgh right away." I have never heard him sound so concerned for Mom.

"I'll text you the address, Dad. Thanks."

"Don't worry, Nora. I'll be there soon."

It was around 10 p.m. when Dad arrived at the hospital. He was looking for Mom as if he hadn't seen her in years. His eyes were red and his face looked pale. I briefed him about the situation. Neil got coffee for us, but neither of us was really feeling like it.

I asked Violet to go back and rest. She promised to visit whenever she had time. Dad insisted that I go home, freshen up, and get some rest as he wanted to be there with Mom. I refused and asked him to go home instead, but he didn't listen to me at all, and I had to leave. Neil gave me a ride home in his car. I was too embarrassed to say anything. The awkward silence between us broke when Neil asked for my phone.

"Give me your phone?"

"Sorry, why?" I asked hesitantly.

"I'll save my contact number in your phone so that you can call me in case you need help, anytime."

He took my phone and saved his number in my emergency contacts.

"Don't think too much when you get home. Get some good sleep. I'll pick you up in the morning. Meet me at the parking lot by seven, I'll take you to the hospital."

"No, thanks. You've already done a lot for me. I'll take a cab." I declined his offer politely.

"It's not only about you. Yes, I want to be there for you, but I want to check up on your mom, too."

"You really don't have to..." Before I could finish, the car stopped. I got off.

"Good night. I'll park the car. You go ahead and rest. See you in the morning and..." He paused for a moment. *"Take care."* He said softly.

"Thanks, good night," I answered.

I watched his car disappear and walked toward the apartment.

I couldn't stop worrying about Mom, but Dad's concern for her gave me hope. I took a shower, brewed some chamomile tea to relax before going to bed. I called Dad and asked him if he had eaten anything at all. He said that he only had some coffee and was not hungry. I told him that I would visit in the morning, take a day off to be with mom, and that he should get some rest while I stay with mom.

8

It's been a week, and Mom didn't wake up. Dad and I have been taking turns to stay with her, and I've realized one thing during this time that even though they never show, they do care for each other, or maybe they needed a little push to put in some effort. Neil has been chauffeuring me to the hospital every day. He has been there with me all week, checking up on me, to see if I eat or sleep well. I am afraid of all of this. What if I get attached to him? Deep down, I feel good to have someone by my side, to care for me, but this doesn't mean that I can rely on him like forever. All these questions keep hitting me from time to time. Violet visits the hospital every day after work. She has been sick worried about me because she knows how much I care for my parents, even though I never show it.

I was almost ready to leave for the hospital, and Neil was waiting outside to pick me up. Right then, my phone rang and it was Dad.

"Hello, Dad. Do you need anything? I am about to leave in a minute."

I heard him crying. My heart sank.

"Dad, what happened? Mom's okay, right?" It took a lot of strength for me to speak. It felt like someone was strangling me.

"She is awake. Emma woke up. Come quickly, she is asking for you." He continued to cry.

"I am coming right away, Dad. I am coming." I picked up my jacket and ran to the parking lot where I meet Neil every day. I saw him waiting for me, and as he looked at me, his expression changed. He stopped smiling and seemed concerned as I almost tripped in front of him.

"Hey, hey. What happened?" He held my hand. *"Why the rush, and why are you crying?"*

"Dad called. Mom woke up." I finally spoke after a pause and started weeping.

"That's great. See, I told you everything would be fine. Calm down. Let's hurry to the hospital." He hugged me with much excitement, and I was so overwhelmed that I put my arms around him tightly. We stayed like that until I stopped crying.

We reached the hospital and I sprinted to see Mom. I saw Dad caressing her hair, and they both were smiling. Just the sight of them being like this together made me feel so relieved. I went inside the room and stood beside Mom near the bed.

"You're feeling okay, Mom?"

"I am all right." Her voice was feeble. She smiled.

Neil was standing outside, watching us from there. I turned to him and signaled him to come in, but he refused and mouthed that he would wait outside instead. I was there with my mom for some time and then went out looking for Neil. I couldn't find him anywhere nearby, so I walked to the garden and found him sitting on a bench under a tree. The sun was shining brightly.

The faded sunlight falling on him through the tree created an orb around him, or it seemed so in my eyes. He looked like an angel, which he actually was for me. I wanted to look at him like this forever, but he seemed to be waiting for me impatiently. He looked at his watch, at the sky, and then his eyes searched through the crowd. He turned back and saw me. His face lit up as if he had found something precious. He waved at me, I walked toward him, and sat beside him.

"How's she?"

"She looks good. The doctor said that we can take her home tomorrow and continue with the medication. We just need to visit for regular follow-ups."

"That's great!" He answered.

"Thank you, Neil." I looked him in the eyes. *"Thanks for everything you have done for me all this time, I owe you one."*

"Why does it feel like you want me to leave?" He raised an eyebrow and asked.

"No, you got it wrong. I've always wanted to thank you, but never had the right time."

"Okay." He said and paused for a moment, thinking deeply.

"Then, how about a dinner?"

"Dinner?" I repeated.

"Yes, let's have dinner together this Sunday, and I'll consider this as your thanks."

"But…?"

"Stop! Before you say anything, just remember that you owe me one. First things first. Now that your mom is okay, let's take her home, and you will meet me on Sunday at "The Fine Dine". I'll be there by eight." Before I could say anything, he stood up, grinned, and walked away with a cheerful smile, leaving me confused, thinking about what to do.

***

Violet was at the hospital looking for me. I was in the cafeteria, lost in my thoughts.

"You disappeared again," Violet said, sliding into the chair across from me with two iced lattes in hand. I offered her a weak smile. *"Just needed some space."*

She arched a brow. *"You always need space when things start to feel... safe. What is it this time? Is it about Neil?"*

I flinched and looked at her with surprise, *"Huh?"*

"So, it is about him, the sweet neighbor."

I looked away, tightening my fingers around the glass.

She sighed, softer now. *"You do this, Nora. You pull back the second someone gets close. Don't think too much because overthinking always ruins everything. Just live with what you have today, forgetting about everything that has happened in the past. I think he likes you, Nora. I could see it in his eyes."*

"What are you talking about? We're just…" I stopped without finishing my sentence.

"You are…? Just friends? Neighbors? I think it's something more, Nora. You just need to feel it."

"He's too kind. And I sometimes don't know what to do with it. He has seen me at my worst, which I hate." I blinked back the sting in my eyes.

Violet added gently, *"Nora, you are not that scared little girl anymore, and he is not how you think every man is like. I can see that he treats you differently. And he is definitely a lot better than that moron, Luke."*

I caught my breath. That name, that comparison. But Violet didn't look away. She held her gaze with fierce loyalty. *"You're allowed to love and be loved. Don't be harsh on yourself. I want you to be happy with someone who will treat you right, and trust me, you deserve it."*

I looked down, tears finally slipping. Not from pain, but for punishing myself for the mistakes I never made.

9

It was 'the day' when I had to join Neil for dinner. I didn't realize it was already 7 pm, and I promised to meet him at eight. One by one, I started throwing my dresses on the bed, looking for something nice to wear. Several minutes passed, but I still couldn't find the right dress for me. I picked up the black full-length dress that I haven't tried since I bought it. *When nothing makes sense, always choose a black dress.* I thought to myself, proudly. I chose simple jewelry and makeup to go with the dress as I wanted to make it look effortless and elegant. I made sure that Mom was okay, kissed her forehead, and told her that I would get back as early as possible, to which she said that I could take my time and smiled.

Dad was out to get some fruit, and he was about to return home, so I started to leave. By the time I left home, it was 7:45 pm. I walked across the street to hail a cab. I kept walking to find a ride and reached a park that was close to my neighborhood. I was in the bus station and could see the park from there. I was waiting to get a bus or a taxi, anything at all, as I was already late. While standing there, I glanced at the park and smiled, watching a group of kids playing and running around. Suddenly, I spotted two familiar faces. It was Luke and Tira. Luke hugged her playfully. The mere sight of this shook me to the core.

Tira was an assistant editor at the publishing firm where Luke and I were interns. I knew that he was someone who could take advantage of people's feelings, but I never figured out from his puppy face that he could use personal connections to get his way up. I was too stunned to see them together. It's been over a year since I last saw him. My eyes were filled with tears when I realized that Tira was pregnant. Luke put his hand on her belly, said something to her, and they both laughed. They looked so happy together. Their rings flashed, blinding my eyes.

I couldn't move a muscle. I couldn't believe my eyes. He had moved on and was happy in his life, whereas I was still there, standing where I was, trying to forget about him and blaming myself for everything. I felt so stupid at that moment to even have thought to forgive him if he came to apologize to me someday. *What was I even thinking? How could I be such a fool? He doesn't love me or need me; he never did.* I started reminiscing about the time when I fell in love with him. I started walking wherever my feet took me to and suddenly it started drizzling. In no time, I found myself crying. I had nowhere to go, so I just walked anywhere.

This feeling was something I'd never imagined it would be like. I thought I would be okay if I ever saw Luke with someone else, but it was not how things turned out. I wasn't prepared for this, at least not at this moment.

My phone was continuously ringing, but I couldn't look into my bag for it. My head was spinning, and I couldn't hear or think of anything at all. I just walked and walked and then reached a place I wasn't familiar with. It was a small playground near a residential area. It was still drizzling. By walking this much, I was almost wet from head to toe. I stopped and sat on a bench in the playground. I have been crying continuously.

I blamed myself for everything that has happened to me. I didn't realize how much time had passed by then. I was still sitting there and weeping. Someone walked and stood in front of me while I was looking at the ground.

"So, here you are." His voice was desperate. He was gasping for air as if he had been running. I recognized his voice immediately, but couldn't see him clearly because of all the crying and rain. Neil put his jacket over me and knelt to the ground.

"Are you all right? What happened? I've been looking for you everywhere. What are you doing here?" He asked each question with so much concern. He was damp himself, yet he was worried about me. He put his hand on my face and wiped off a tear and then another. He then leaned forward and put his hands on mine.

"If you don't want to say anything to me right now, it's okay. I won't ask you anything anymore until you tell me why I had to find you here in this situation." He stood up and asked me to leave with him, but I sat there like a statue.

"Get up, Nora. Let's go home." He spoke.

"Come with me, I'll take you home." He said again.

I still didn't move, but I could feel the frustration growing in his voice.

"What's wrong with you, Nora? We promised to have dinner together, and you stood me up. You didn't answer my calls; Violet has been calling you, and she even called your mom. No one knows where you are. I have been looking for you everywhere, and then I find you here like this, and you are not telling me what has happened, and you are not coming with me either. What do you want me to do?" He spoke loudly in desperation.

"Leave me alone," I said, mouthing the words slowly with a cracked voice.

"What? You want me to leave? You want me to leave you here, like this?" He asked amusingly.

I took a moment to speak, *"Yes, please leave me alone. I want to be alone right now. Why do you even care? Who are you? What am I to you? Just leave. Everyone leaves me, so why can't you do the same? Please, leave."* I yelled at him.

"I am not going to leave you. Do you hear me? I don't know what has happened, but I want to let you know that I will always be there with you, ALWAYS. So, stop making yourself miserable. You never try to look at things in a bright light. You hold on to things too tightly that's gone wrong, but what if, just once, you let go?" He clenched his fist and spoke at the top of his lungs this time.

"Why? But why are you doing this to me? No one cares, and you, too, shouldn't. Just let me be and go home." I shouted and started crying more.

"You want to know why? Because-because I love you, Nora, and everything about you fascinates me." I looked at him, confused. His eyes were red and filled with tears. His fist was so tightly closed that I could see his veins clearly.

"And because I love you so much, my heart aches to see you like this. Doesn't matter how much you push me away, I won't leave you, never."

My head was blank. I stopped thinking about Luke and Tira. I couldn't understand what was happening and why at that very moment.

"Don't worry. These are my feelings, so no pressure. I had to tell you this just so you know that there is someone who loves you. In fact, there are a lot of people who love you, just look around yourself and try to see, not with your bare eyes but with your loving heart."

He gave me his hand and waited for me to hold it. I hesitated at first, but him being there with me gave me a comforting feeling. His jacket kept me warm in that cold night rain, and my heart wasn't aching anymore. I was rather confused than depressed. I didn't have the strength to think anymore, so I reached out to hold his hand. He drove me home. Silence filled the air. No questions asked, no answers given.

10

I called in sick and didn't go to work the next day.

"NORA??? Where are you? It's thirty past your punch-in time." Mr. Griffin sounded obnoxious as always when I answered his call.

"Morning, Mr. Griffin. I am a bit under the weather, so I called in sick. You know, I don't want to spread the cold to everyone else at work." I said wisely. Mr. Griffin is someone who fears falling sick the most and always keeps a sanitizer with him that he uses every ten minutes. I had to think tactically to get my leave approved.

"Well, then it can't be helped, but I want you to e-mail me the final draft of the proposal that we needed it today." He demanded.

"Sure, I'll do it right away."

I heard the beep and then dead air. He had this habit of disconnecting the call abruptly.

I couldn't bear to face Neil because I felt too awkward after what happened that night. I knew that I might have broken his heart so badly that he would not like the idea of me standing in front of him. So, in order to avoid him, I did all sorts of stupid things like looking out from the balcony to see if he was out there, wearing a cap and black sunglasses, looking around me, and sprinting if I saw anyone walking toward me. I have gone nuts, I know.

I didn't see Neil around lately. It is true that I was indeed avoiding him, but I was worried too. It was a Sunday, so I went to the café to divert my mind from all that had happened

during the last couple of weeks. I ordered a bagel with my usual coffee. I stood there waiting for Alex to bring my order, but too many thoughts kept rushing in. Two weeks have passed, and there is no sign of Neil. It started to worry me more when Alex asked me about Neil.

"Do you know where's Neil? I haven't seen him for weeks. I hope he's okay." Alex enquired.

"I didn't know he was a regular here." I asked curiously.

"What? He visits every Sunday at 10:30 am, just before you come, and always leaves after you. Have you never noticed him before?" Alex's eyes were questioning me desperately.

"What do you mean?" I tried to act calm.

"Neil always asked about you. It seemed from the beginning that he liked you. He used to ask me about your tastes and preferences, what kind of guys you like, he even started ordering the same coffee that you have." Alex told me these details with much excitement.

"How long has it been, all this going on, I mean?"

"About four or five months probably."

Before knowing all this, I was just worried and sad, but all of my concerns turned into surprise, and I began to worry more. There were a lot of questions going on inside my head. *I want to meet Neil. I have so much to ask him.* I left my coffee there and left in a hurry. I could hear Alex's faint voice calling me, *"Nora, where are you going? Your coffee?"* I had no time to even look back and answer. The next thing I remember is that I was standing at Neil's door. It took me a moment of hesitation to ring the doorbell. I did it once, twice, thrice. No one answered.

The only thing I could hear was the sound of the doorbell echoing as if there was just an empty room on the other side. I started looking for my phone in my bag. I dialed his number and waited. *"The number you've called is not available."* It was all I listened to for ten minutes as I called him non-stop, and by the tenth time hearing the same IVR, I started losing my patience. My desperation grew deeper. I had no idea how to get in touch with him, and with this, I realized how little I knew about him, whereas he became a part of my life and knew so many things about me. The only thing I had asked him was what he did for a living, and he responded that he worked as a senior journalist in a media firm in Charlotte Square. I have never asked him about his family or friends. Shame filled me as I realized how selfish I've been toward him and how selfless he's been all this time.

It made me compare myself to Luke. I have always needed help from Neil, and he was there, but when he expressed his feelings for me, I disregarded everything. I did not even consider his feelings once since then. I collapsed on the floor outside his apartment, leaning on his door, buried my face in my hands, and sobbed for so long that I don't remember how much time had passed.

11

I still can't believe that it's already been a month since Neil disappeared just like that. No goodbye, no farewell, no news from him. Each day has been suffocating for me. I have been waiting and waiting, as there was nothing else I could do. All I had with me was his wonderful memories- mischievous, blissful, and warm. On the day my mom was hospitalized, Neil took me to his favorite place to calm me down from all the stress and crying. It was close to our place and on the way home, with just a small diversion. He stopped his car mid-way on an uphill road and parked on the curb. When I asked him why he stopped there, he said, *"I want to show you something. This is my secret place."*

We got out of the car and stood on the pavement. He looked at me and said, *"Close your eyes and feel the air."* I looked at him, surprised, and hesitated. It looked childish to me.

"Do it." He insisted.

"I come here often when I'm exhausted and overwhelmed with emotions. This place gives me a serene feeling, positivity, and hope to carry on even if things get hard."

I closed my eyes and felt the cool breeze hitting my face. It turned a little windy in a moment, blocking all the thoughts running wild inside my head. I could feel my hair flowing along the wind, and I imagined myself in one of those movie scenes where the female lead gets all dressed up and the male lead looks at her with love, and her hair dances with the wind, making her shine from every angle. I don't know why, but I felt as if Neil was staring at me all this time, but it didn't make me uncomfortable at all, instead, it felt reassuring as if he was watching out for me.

"Now, open your eyes and look there." He pointed his finger at the setting sun.

I opened my eyes and looked at the beautiful orangish colored ball that was still shining bright and giving light. Half of it was hidden behind the horizon. Its rays are spreading through the sky, spearing the clouds. It was less windy now, and the breeze was cooler than before.

"Look at everything around you. Look, those birds, they are going back home. The trees stand tall and strong. The clouds are in different sizes and shapes, and that— the main character of the story— The Sun. How beautiful it looks even when it is dying, because we all know that it is going to rise again in the morning, and this is not the end. The world will be filled up with its rays, and everything will light up again. So, smile when you want to, laugh when you want to, get mad if you're frustrated, ask for help when you need it, don't think too much- why, what, how. Pretending to be strong is a foolish thing to do. Your emotions will only eat you up from inside if you don't show them."

I looked at him, and his eyes were saying it all, yet I chose to deny it. He continued, *"We all go through tough times, but thinking about others before yourself is stupid. You can always count on me. Just think of me as your diary, use me as you want. Tell me all about you, and I will keep them to myself. Talk to me if things get hard. Do whatever you want to, and I'll join you if it feels lonely or a silly thing to do. Don't care about anything else. Make yourself your first priority."* He took a step closer, looked into my eyes, and said, *"I want you to be happy. I want you to leave all your worries behind and do what your heart says without thinking too much, and I promise to be there with you, always."*

My heart raced. Neither of us blinked for a while, and then there was a loud horn by a car that broke our stare game.

Thinking all of this gave me a vivid flashback while I was standing at the same place, 'his secret place'. I have been going there every day for over two weeks. I come back after the sun has set, and when it gets dark, hoping to see Neil there. *I would yell at him, maybe even slap him hard, and ask him where he had been, why he did not inform me of anything before leaving.* People say that memories fade away with time, but it was totally opposite with me. With each day passing, my feelings for him grew intense. I knew that there was something different about missing him so badly.

I wanted to divert my mind from all that was happening to me, so I decided to go to the library. I asked Mrs. Hughes to suggest a book that would make me feel better, as I was feeling low. Mrs. Hughes has been working in the library for twenty years. She was in her mid-fifties, short, very talkative, and wore a pair of big round glasses. She jotted down something on a sticky note and handed it to me. She looked at my diary and said, *"Oh, you still carry your diary with you. That's great. Only if he didn't find it that day..."* I looked at her with confusion and scratched my forehead.

"I don't understand. I collected it from the library, you know all about it." I spoke.

"Well, actually, a young man found your diary that day when you forgot it in the library. He was very respectful and handsome." She rubbed her nose and adjusted her glasses.

"Oh, right. I remember now." She said loudly, and everyone stared at her strangely.

"I am sorry." She mouthed the words and continued, *"It was your birthday in January, I can't seem to remember the date, sorry darling."*

"15 January," I answered, interrupting her.

"Oh, yes. Right. It was 15 January, on your birthday, when you brought me cupcakes. They were lovely, I must say." She seemed to have lost track of the point that we were on, so I gave her a dense look.

"Oh, I am sorry, dear. So, where was I, yes... You were sitting at that table." She pointed her finger toward the desk that I always occupy. *"That day, you looked quite upset, and you also forgot your diary there on that table. Then, there was a young man who found it. What was his name again? Ah-Nate, no-no. Um-Neil. Yes, his name was Neil."* Hearing his name shook me. My heart was beating fast.

"Neil? Are you sure? His name was Neil?" I wanted to confirm what I heard.

"Yes, dear. His name was Neil. He looked well-groomed and he was this tall." She used her hand to tell me how tall he was.

"I saw him reading the diary for a couple of hours with mixed emotions, so I thought it was his diary, but then he came to me and asked me to give him your information so that he could give you the diary personally. You know that we can't give out our members' personal information, so I asked him to give it to us, and that we would inform you to come and collect it from the library, and then I gave you a call regarding the same." She said all of this in one breath and let out a big sigh.

"Oh, there's one thing that I couldn't understand. He knew your name already, and he asked me if you were Nora, who moved here from Preston."

I was too stunned to speak. Things can't get more entangled than this. How did he know my name? Why did he read my diary, and if he did read it, then it means that he knew everything about me from the beginning.

"Neil was here the next day when you came and took the diary with you. I saw him standing and waiting patiently for you since we opened the library." She added another line.

I stood there silently. I felt a mild pain in my chest. I collected all the information and put it together. Meeting him in the café was not a coincidence. He's had feelings for me long before that. He has known me when I never knew someone called Neil existed around me. He read my diary, which means he knows about my childhood, my family, my failed love, and my pathetic life. He knows what kind of a pathetic loser I am, and yet he chose to be with me. *I don't deserve his love and kindness.* I repeated this line until I reached home and surrendered to my bed.

12

The holiday season was around the corner. There were lights everywhere. Streets were lit up with smiling faces, and the kids started writing their wishes. The smell of happiness and love could be felt along with the essence of winter, although it is usually cold here in Edinburgh. I always wait for the holiday season to see how it spreads the magic of joy in the air. A whole season has passed, and I have still been waiting for him. Was he always this cruel to leave without a word? It hurts me so much to think that I had the chance, but I was never willing to know about him. I have tried all that I could, but there was no way to reach out to him. I looked for all the media firms in Charlotte Square, and when I got to know one firm where he worked, I was told that he quit his job for personal reasons. *Could that personal reason be me?* I still come to see the sunset every day, praying that he comes back. I looked at the sky and started to think about my time spent here.

This thought amuses me every time. When I moved to Edinburgh, I was lonely and had only one friend who was like a soul sister to me. Later, I met Alex at the café and we became good friends. I crossed paths with Luke briefly, who turned my life upside down but taught me an unforgettable lesson. I thought that I would never feel this way for anyone ever, but then Neil walked into my life, and things changed. My life only received rainfall, but he came with a huge umbrella to save me from getting soaked. Now, mom and dad are also here with me, and the best thing is that they are both happy.

I remember Neil had said that I have a lot of people who love me. Things seem to be much better now, but I still feel a weird kind of emptiness and can't get rid of this feeling.

I am still afraid to admit my feelings, but I don't know how long I will be able to keep this. I miss him, I do. *I want you here with me. I have so many things to ask you and so much to tell you. Please come back. I really miss you.* I closed my eyes and prayed earnestly, looking at the sky, standing at the same place where Neil and I were standing when he brought me here for the first time. Every word he said to me that day replayed inside my head like I was listening to my favorite sad song, where the lyrics tell the story that it was a dream, and that we would never meet again, and that night was our last goodbye. I teared up, shut my eyes tightly, hoping to push the flashbacks away.

A warm drop of tear slowly moved from my eye and went all the way through my cheek when it felt like a voice called me. My thoughts completely vanished. I stopped thinking and only focused on the voice and the warm tear near my lips. I recognized the voice, but I still wasn't sure if this was real or if I was just hearing things because I was thinking too much.

I was afraid to turn back to see who was there because if there was no one, then it would shatter me, and I would break down, as I had already had enough being patient. I gathered the courage and looked back. His image was blurry due to tears in my eyes. I wiped them off to see clearly if what I was looking at was real or just a dream.

It was him. It was Neil, standing a few feet away from me. He looked pale, and his eyes were dull. He seemed thin and weak. We were both standing still, looking at each other. No one moved. No one spoke.

At some point in time, we all feel that life is unfair. But, don't you think if life was fair for all of us, then would we ever appreciate the good things in life? If we got everything without even asking for it, without praying for it, then would we ever acknowledge its worth? Sadness is equally important in life for us to understand what happiness feels like. We cannot see the rainbow until it rains.

NORA & NEIL
Coincidentally?

Part Two
Neil

1

Isn't it amazing when things that are bound to happen only happen after you have prayed with full determination, and then all of it feels fruitful and your heart is filled with contentment, finally. I lived with my aunt in Preston. She adopted me when I was ten, after my parents passed away in an accident. After graduating from high school, I moved to London for further studies, and then settled in Edinburgh after getting a permanent position. It was then that I saw Nora. But no, it wasn't the first time I've crossed paths with her. She wouldn't even know if I told her because back then, someone called Neil never existed in her world.

The first time I saw Nora was when I was in my freshman year in high school. I was in the debate club, and there was a cultural fest coming up, so everyone was busy preparing for it, and I volunteered for the backstage crew in hopes of making a few friends. I was always treated like an outcast because no one wanted to befriend a nerd. It's nothing to be appreciated for. Everyone envied the kid who topped the class. So, I changed myself a bit, just to look cool. I started wearing casuals rather than formals more often, and learned the slang that people of my age used. In reality, I was just desperate to make some friends, trying to fit in.

It was the day before the fest. We wrapped up after the rehearsals. I almost reached the parking lot when it hit me that I didn't have my phone with me. I searched for it in my pockets and my bag, but it wasn't there, then I realized that I must have left it in the auditorium, so I ran back. When I reached the auditorium, I saw that the lights were switched on and a slow contemporary music was playing. I continued with my search and found my phone near the box of props. I was sure that I had double checked everything before leaving and that I had switched off the lights and unplugged the speaker, then how did this happen? I moved toward the stage to see who was there, and I was mesmerized by what I saw. A girl in a white T-shirt, a pair of baggy trousers, and a checkered shirt wrapped around her waist, her hair made up in a messy bun, swayed and swirled on the stage in the spotlight. I realized she was barefoot when she gently kicked into the thin air. She twisted her body in such a flexible way that she looked fragile and made me want to hold her and protect her.

The best thing was that she didn't skip a beat. When she took the final twist and stood straight, her bun loosened, and now her hair was flowing down her neck till her waist, swaying like a pendulum. She was breathing fast. Then she bowed to an empty audience. The show was over, and it somehow disappointed me. She stood still, catching her breath, and wiped off the sweat from her forehead with her sleeves. She then took the hairband from her wrist and tied a ponytail, collecting her hair from all sides.

She sat on the floor beside her bag, took out a water bottle, and gulped till the last drop. She picked up her shoes, tied them tightly, grabbed her bag, and was all

set to go. I hid myself to save her from the embarrassment of having someone watching her perform or I could say that I was afraid to go in front of her. She turned off the music and lights and left, wiping off the sweat from her face. I took out a copy of the list of participants from my bag to check who she was, as I did not see her during any of the rehearsals. I searched for any new entries in the list, but there was none.

Who was she? She left me guessing.

***

It was the fest day. Everyone was excited and looking forward to the event, but my eyes were only searching for that girl in the crowd. I was backstage helping the performers, hoping to see her once again. One by one, the participants were done, but there was no sign of the girl I was desperately waiting for. I enquired here and there, but it all seemed futile. I was disheartened, but I made it my mission to find her and prove to myself that she was real and not a ghost.

For the next few days, I looked for her everywhere, and it was very unfortunate that I couldn't find her. I started losing hope, and my search mission was nearing the end. I wandered the cafeteria during lunch, scanned every face in the classrooms I passed, and even lingered longer than usual near the auditorium. It was as if she had vanished into thin air. I was in the library looking for a book in the aisle of shelves and picked up the book to see if it was from the author that I wanted to read. Right then, I felt someone standing next to me. Suddenly, my book was taken away by force from me.

"Can I have it, if you're done checking it out?" A voice asked.

I turned to look at this unfriendly tone, and I froze.

It was her. She opened the book and seemed completely lost in the pages. I didn't move, thinking that if this isn't real, then she might disappear. I swallowed a lump then cleared my throat, *"Yes."*

"Okay, thanks." She said and walked away.

I stood there watching her walk away with the book. She went to the librarian to get the book for her. I admired her from there, standing still, when she tucked a strand of hair behind her ear. I felt an odd sense of relief knowing that she was real. She slipped the book into her bag and left. I quickly followed her, keeping a safe distance. I trailed after her, weaving through the students in the hallway, not wanting to lose her again.

Who was she? Why did it feel like I've been waiting for this moment? Why did my heart feel at peace just by her presence?

I didn't have the answers, but one thing was certain that I wasn't going to let her disappear again. Since then, I followed her and always watched her from afar without her knowing that there was someone who looked at her and smiled.

2

I became a silent spectator in her life. I was always there, just a few steps behind- watching her as she tied her hair before her creative writing class, smiling when she argued with her friend passionately about a book that she read, and stealing glances when she sat by the library window, lost in her world. I have always loved reading, but seeing her love for books grew an intense sense of connection with books in me. I never said a word, even when we walked past each other in the hallways, when she stood beside me in the lunch queue, and certainly not when she leaned close to her only friend, whispering secrets that I would never hear.

By the time high school ended, I had memorized every detail of her presence but had never been a part of it. Then life happened. London came calling me. I left without a goodbye- after all, what was there to say? That I had spent years loving her from the shadows? That I had written a thousand letters in my mind? That I had wished, more than anything, for the courage to tell her?

London was fast-paced, thrilling, a city that kept me busy enough to forget her, almost. But on quiet nights, when the rain drummed against my window, I thought of her. Did she ever wonder about me? Probably not. After some time, I moved to Edinburgh. A permanent position, a stable life. The city was quieter, wrapped in cobbled streets and a different kind of charm. But even here, amidst the history and the cold wind that rushed through the streets, she lingered in my thoughts every now and then.

And then one day, when I was in the library getting a new book to read, I saw her as she walked into the library, handed a box to the librarian, and walked toward me. She sat right in front of me. I couldn't believe what I saw. *Is it really her? Am I hallucinating? Maybe it's someone else.* But then she took out a diary from her bag and placed it on the desk. It was the same diary that she's always had, even during high school. She scribbled in it most of the time. Then, she did it, something that could make me fall all over again every time she does it. She collected her hair from all sides and made a messy bun.

I have never expected to see her again. Not here, not after all these years. Yet, there she was, sitting in front of me, completely unaware of my existence. She still looked beautiful, as if time had barely touched her. *How do you speak to someone who once meant everything to you? What do you tell someone who doesn't even know that you exist in this world, observing them quietly?*

A couple of hours passed by just like a few minutes. I was so lost in admiring her and delighted by her presence that I didn't notice she had left her diary on the desk. I stared at the small leather-bound diary on the table and hovered my fingers around it. I wanted to grab it and run after her, but something stopped me. I picked up the diary, getting tempted to read it, but a part of me wanted to stop, to respect her privacy. But I was drowning in curiosity and nostalgia.

I have followed her for years, and I have always wanted to know everything about her so that I can give her the feeling of comfort and peace. Before I realized it, I had flipped it open. I skimmed through the words, and in an instant, I was pulled into her world.

Some pages were filled with hurried scribbles while others were carefully penned. Some entries made me smile, while most of them held questions, confessions of confusion, and pain. Then reality struck. I shouldn't have read it. Snapping the diary, I exhaled sharply, guilt and longing crashing into me at once. I slowly walked with the diary, carrying the guilt of reading it in my heart, to the short, middle-aged lady and asked her for Nora's address, but she politely declined, repeating the library rules about not giving out any personal information.

I left the diary with her and waited at the library the next day to see her just one more time, just the way I did in school. I was eagerly waiting for her, and my heart was at peace when she came to collect her diary. I started frequenting the library just to see her once again, and then once again.

I moved to an apartment for an easy commute, and I visited a café nearby whenever I had time. The guy who worked there was very friendly, so we connected well and became friends quickly, and this gave me another reason to visit the café more often, as I didn't know anyone in Edinburgh then. And then one day, while I was sitting in the café, I saw Nora. It was a Sunday. She ordered her coffee, enjoyed the view outside, scribbled something in her diary, and left. Later, when I enquired casually with Alex, the guy who worked at the café, I learned that it was her Sunday routine, so I started to visit the café every Sunday morning. Just looking at her face made my day.

I still regret our first encounter that made me look like a snob in her eyes, and so the second one. Our second encounter was in front of her apartment, or I can say my apartment, maybe our apartment. Well, one thing is for sure that I may have gone overboard that day, but I was just trying to tell her that she needed to see things differently, never mind.

3

It occurred to me why I had never gathered the courage to talk to her, to get closer to her. The fear of rejection, the uncertainty of her feelings, and the possibility of ruining whatever fragile connection we could have. These thoughts always held me back. But now, as I stood in the dimly lit diner, waiting for her to come, it all seemed foolish. I asked Nora out for dinner; it was just a friendly dinner date and nothing else, but I have always wanted to tell her how I feel about her. I spent a couple of days planning this evening.

Choosing the perfect table, the perfect food, and music that suits her taste. The diner wasn't too fancy, but it had character, a warmth that I thought she would appreciate. I made sure everything was just right- the soft glow of the lights, the quiet hum of the music in the background, the best dishes on the menu. I wanted everything to be so perfect that when I finally told her how I felt, the moment would be something she would remember.

I imagined how it would go. She would walk in, looking effortlessly beautiful, her presence enough to make my heart race. We would talk, maybe laugh, and somewhere in between, I would find the courage to tell her how I had admired her from a distance, how I had replayed every small interaction in my mind, searching for signs that she might feel the same way, for years since high school.

But she didn't come.

Minutes turned to hours, and the untouched food on the table grew cold. I checked my phone more times than I cared to admit, hoping for a message, an excuse, anything. But there was nothing. At first, I tried to justify it. Maybe she got caught up in something urgent. Maybe she is late. But as time dragged on, the reality sank in that she wasn't coming. I still made an effort to call her and remind her about our dinner in case she had forgotten, but she didn't answer my call. I wasn't sure what hurt more: the fact that she didn't come or the fact that I had let myself hope.

I had spent so long convincing myself that I wasn't good enough for her, but tonight, I had dared to believe otherwise. I had dared to imagine a different version of this evening, one where she showed up, where she smiled, where she listened as I poured my heart out. And now, all I was left with was an empty chair across from me.

The waitress came by, offering me a look of sympathy as she cleared the plates.

"Would you like anything else?" She asked softly.

I shook my head. *"No, I think I'm done, thank you."*

As I stood up to leave, I received a call from Violet asking if Nora was with me, as she had not been answering her calls. I told her that she was supposed to have dinner with me, but she never came. Violet sounded quite concerned when she told me that Nora never ignores anyone's calls or texts, but she has not even once responded all evening.

I felt a bit anxious as Violet called me again after a minute, telling me that she had called Nora's mother, and she is not home. She left, saying that she was going to meet me. *If she left home to meet me, then where is she? Why didn't she come? I hope nothing bad happened to her.* I wanted to think positively, but I was getting more and more anxious.

I started looking for her on the streets. The diner was not too far from our apartment, so I ran checking all the cabs standing in a row and also those that passed by. It was ten, and I was extremely worried as there was no trace of her. I was exhausted from all the running, and on top of that, it started raining. I was soaked in the rain, and right then, I saw a small playground near me. I walked a few steps and, after looking closely, I saw a woman sitting on a bench. I hoped for it to be Nora, so I walked closer and to my surprise, it was her. I tried to catch my breath and took a sigh of relief that she didn't seem to be hurt, but it broke my heart to see her crying, although I had no idea of what exactly had happened.

4

The sun was dipping below the horizon in a quiet farewell. The cold breeze carried the scent of Earth. Nora stood at the edge, her arms wrapped around herself, staring at the fading sun. This place had once been painted with positivity, smiles, and whispered dreams. Now, it held only silence and longing. I was surprised to see her there. Her lips moved in a silent prayer, but I wasn't sure what she was praying for so earnestly. I uttered under my breath, *"Nora"*. Her shoulders stiffened and her breath hitched, and then she turned sharply. Standing a few feet away, just as I remember her- her eyes holding a storm, her face carrying the weight of something unspoken. The wind ruffled her hair, and the setting sun cast a golden outline around her, as if she had stepped out of a dream.

I wasn't expecting to see her here of all the places. I walked toward her slowly, and I could see her breathing fast and shuddering. I was now standing in front of her. Her lips parted, her brows furrowing.

"Where were you?" She spoke in a cracked voice.

The words cut through the air like a blade. Her voice trembled, not just with anger but with something deeper, something broken.

"You disappeared. You disappeared just like that. No calls, no messages, no goodbye. Do you have any idea what that did to me?" I hated myself to hear her cracked voice.

"Nora-" I started, but she didn't let me finish.

"I thought something happened to you. I thought-" She swallowed hard, blinking back tears. *"I thought you were dead."*

I flinched. God, I wanted to say something, to take it all back, to tell her that I never meant to hurt her. But what excuse could justify months of silence? So, I told her the truth.

"I didn't have a choice."

"There's always a choice." She shot back, her voice was sharp.

"Even if it was just a single text- something. Anything to let me know you were alive."

I clenched my jaw, exhaling sharply.

"My aunt was dying, Nora." She froze.

"I got a call that night after I dropped you home." I continued; my voice was quieter now.

"I took the first flight that I could to reach Preston on time. She had a liver failure; we needed a donor as soon as possible. Her husband and son were neither a match for a donor, so I wanted to give it a try because she was slipping away. I got tested and fortunately, I was a match. So, we had the surgery planned for the next day. She recovered in a few days, while it took me months due to some complications post-surgery. But all this was nothing compared to what she has done for me. My aunt is the only family I have. She adopted me after my parents passed away. She took care of a kid who was devastated and lost. She has been both a mother and a father to me. I would've done anything to bring her back to life, even if it meant for me to die."

Her eyes softened, but I couldn't stop now.

"I wanted to call you." I admitted. *"So many times... I was dying to hear your voice. Trust me, but my situation didn't allow me. And then I didn't know if my coming back would even matter to you."* I swallowed hard, meeting her gaze.

"I was scared, Nora. I was scared that you'd have forgotten me. That we'd become strangers again, and I didn't have the strength to take it."

She let out a sharp breath, her fingers curling into fists.

"Why didn't you trust me enough to tell me?" She whispered.

I closed my eyes for a moment. I had asked myself the same thing a hundred times.

"Because I didn't know you'd wait for me." She laughed softly, bitterly.

"Of course, I waited. I hated you for leaving, Neil, but I hated myself for never giving up on you and for feeling for you, each day, more and more."

Something in me shattered. I stepped closer, hesitantly. *"And now?"*

She looked up at me, her eyes glistened when she reached for me. Her hands found my face, her touch hesitant at first, then firm— like she was trying to convince herself that I was real. I let out a breath I didn't know I was holding, my hands onto her like she was the only real thing in that moment.

"Thank you for coming back. Your absence made me realize what you meant to me. Don't disappear again." She whispered; her voice barely audible over the wind.

"I won't." I looked into her eyes and confirmed.

And then she fell into my arms. I held her tightly like I'd never let her go.

"Are you feeling any better now?" She asked with concern.

"More than I've ever been," I replied happily.

The sky had surrendered to twilight, the last traces of gold fading into a deep, endless blue. The wind whispered through the trees, the leaves rustling, but all I could hear was the sound of her breathing- shaky, uneven, real.

Nora was in my arms.

5

For a long time, neither of us moved. I could feel her fingers curled into my shirt, gripping me like she was afraid that I'd disappear again. And maybe, in some twisted way, I was afraid too, thinking that this was a dream, that I'd wake up to an empty night, to an emptier life. But it was all real. She was here, and so was I. She pulled back slightly, just enough to look up at me. Her eyes searched mine, as if trying to piece together the time we had lost, but with curiosity as if it was looking for an answer.

"Did you know me before we met at the coffee shop?" She interrogated.

I flinched, but I think it was time that I should tell her everything.

"Yes, I have known you for years," I answered.

"How many years?"

"I have watched you transform from a fragile young lady to a strong, independent woman."

She widened her eyes and stared at me.

"What—what do you mean?" Her curiosity crossed all limits this time.

"The first time I saw you was when you were dancing in the auditorium of your high school just before the school fest. After you left, it took me about two weeks to find you. I looked for you everywhere, and then I saw you in the library one day. From that moment onwards, I followed you everywhere like your shadow. I observed and noted every detail. When you smiled, when you looked sad, when you seemed lost and annoyed, and what you always did to your hair, trying to make a bun that always turned out messy. Then, after graduating, I moved to London temporarily, and then came to Edinburgh earlier last year to settle down when I saw you at the library. You were always on my mind even when I never saw you, but the moment I saw you here, my heart was at peace, and all those feelings that never died turned more intense."

She looked at me with teary eyes.

"How can someone love with such determination? I have never believed in true love, but you changed my mind, and I think it was all because of your constant efforts and unwavering feelings."

"Yes, Nora. I have never ever thought to spend my life with anyone else if it wasn't you, because you make me feel great, and I am happy when I'm with you. A part of me always had the faith in my prayers that someday you would acknowledge my feelings."

The wind howled around us, and she shivered slightly. Without thinking, I pulled her closer, my arms wrapping around her like I could shield her from everything I had put her through and that she had suffered all her life.

"You owe me, you know?" She muttered against my chest. I smiled, resting my chin lightly on top of her head. *"I know."*

"I waited every single day", she continued, *"You have months of making up to do."*

"And I have waited to be like this with you, even before I knew what love was. So, I'll start making up for it now."

I pulled back slightly, tilting her chin up so she'd look at me. She raised a brow and asked, *"How?"*

I didn't answer. Instead, I lifted my hand and gently wiped away the stray tear on her cheek, letting my fingers linger for just a second longer than necessary. Then I did what I had wanted to do since the moment she turned around.

I kissed her. Soft, slow, a silent promise between us. I felt her melt into me, her fingers tightening in my shirt as she kissed me back, as if to say, *"You're late, but you're here."* And I was.

When we finally pulled apart, she exhaled a small, almost amused breath.

"You think one kiss makes up for four months of silence?"

I smirked. *"No, but it's a good start."*

She rolled her eyes but didn't pull away, Instead, she rested her forehead against my chest, her voice barely a whisper.

"So, you were indeed a stalker." She smirked, and I laughed.

"I love you." She said softly.

I tightened my hold on her.

"And I've loved you long enough for you to know. Loving you is the only thing I've ever been sure of. Even if I'm lost, I know that I'll always find you because you're my home, Nora. My heart, this life, it all belongs to you, I promise."

The stars began to appear above us, one by one, as if the universe itself was putting things back in place, something that I've yearned for years, with both patience and desperation.

You Make Me Complete

We both lost in love,

Spending the moments together,

Making them special.

Creating memories,

You, caressing my hair

And I, dying to see you smile.

I love it when I see your desperate eyes

Searching for me when I'm not around,

I love it when you say "I love you."

Every time before disconnecting the call.

I love the mornings because waking up beside you gives me peace,

My head on your chest, feeling your heartbeat.

I surrender whole of myself, my love, and my life to you,

You make me complete.

Epilogue

Time moves differently now.

It no longer feels like I'm running from something or trying to fix it. It flows gently. Some days I still wake up with the old weight pressing down on my chest, but I have learned one thing that healing isn't about forgetting.

Here's the most beautiful part of my life.

Neil and I have built a life that doesn't look like a fairytale. It's not perfect. There are dishes left in the sink and burnt dinner. There's silence when either of us is struggling with something. But there's something solid between us; something unshakable- Love.

Yes, love, but also trust, respect, patience, and growth.

Neil never asked me to become someone else. He simply held space for me to become who I was always meant to be. And in that space, I bloomed, slowly, awkwardly, and then fully. I stopped hiding my softness, I stopped pushing love away just because I didn't recognize it at first, I stopped feeling embarrassed asking for help, and shaking off when someone offered to help. I have grown, we have grown together.

And now, there's her.

Our daughter. Her name is 'Aira'. We chose the name together because it means 'of the wind'. Love arrived like a breeze, a heavy storm, unexpected and breathtaking for both of us.

Sometimes I just sit beside her crib and watch her sleep. Her tiny chest rising and falling like she's breathing new meaning into this world for us. Her fingers curl in dreams. Her lashes rest on cheeks that have never known sorrow. She doesn't know yet that life can be cruel. That people can leave. That love, when mishandled, can leave a deep wound and a scar later.

I want her to grow up knowing she is loved, she is safe, wanted, and cherished. I pray, every day, that she never has to learn the harsh reality of life, those lessons the way I did. I want her to know family isn't made of silence or fear, and I feel so fortunate that she has a wonderful father to look up to, who treats her like a princess. I want her to know that she never has to earn affection or question if she belongs. I want to be the mother to her that I've always wanted. Not perfect, not composed, but present, soft, constant.

It scares me sometimes, thinking about the responsibility of rewriting a legacy. The fear of unknowingly passing down the pain that I once carried. But Neil is always there. With his steady presence, with his unwavering belief in me, in us. He reminds us that we are not our pasts. That every day with Aira is a chance to do things differently.

He holds her like she's something sacred. And maybe she is. Maybe she's our second chance at childhood, to relive it with her, to do things that we never got the chance to.

Violet cried the first time she held her.

*"She's so lucky." S*he whispered, brushing Aira's dark hair with trembling fingers.

"She has a mother who sees her. Really sees her."

I cried along with her. Because for the longest time, I didn't believe I'd ever be someone's safe place. I didn't believe I'd be capable of creating a home that wasn't made of silence and shame. But here we are. With a fridge covered in crayon doodles and lullabies echoing in the hallway. With giggles that turn into belly laughs and the smell of warm bottles and bedtime stories read in sleepy voices.

This is what healing can look like.

Not a grand declaration, not a single moment of transformation, but a thousand small ones. Midnight feedings, first steps, Neil gently putting Aira in my arms, like handing me something precious and eternal. I tell her *I love you* every day so that she knows that she is loved. Sometimes you have to say it loudly for the other person to know how you feel about them.

I don't know what kind of woman Aira will grow up to be. I only know that she'll never wonder if she was wanted, she'll never sit in the dark waiting for someone to notice her.

Sometimes, when the house is quiet, when Neil's hand is in mine and Aira is curled in between us, I think back to the girl I used to be; the one who thought love wasn't meant for her. Who believed silence was better than vulnerability.

I wish I could hold her.

I wish I could hug her and tell her that you're going to be okay.

You'll find your way sooner or later. One day, you'll be someone's safe place and your own, too.

This story started with a woman who was afraid to be seen, but it ends with a woman who loves boldly, fully, without apology. And it continues- with Aira. With the little feet that will one day run across the floor. With the laughter that echoes louder than silence ever did. With the life that isn't perfect, but deeply, beautifully real.

Not a coincidence.

Not a fate, either.

Just choice- of a love that is nurtured, and finally, whole.

Author's Note

Writing 'Nora & Neil Coincidentally?' has been an emotional and deeply personal journey for me. This story is not just about two people finding each other— it's about the silent battles we all fight, the scars we carry, and most importantly, the strength it takes to heal.

Love, family, friendship, and our life's struggles shape who we are. Love should be a safe place, but for many, it becomes a source of pain. Family should be where we feel the most protected, but sometimes, it's where our deepest wounds come from. A person should never take their family for granted. The four walls and a ceiling put together can only be called a 'home' when the people living in it love each other, understand, and support each other.

Parenting plays a crucial role in all of this. Children don't choose the families they are born into, yet they suffer the consequences of their parents' actions. Whether through neglect, indifference, lack of love, or mostly through the negativity they get to see between their parents. This trauma doesn't fade with time— it lingers, shaping how they see themselves and the world. They become reserved, hesitant to trust, and afraid of being hurt, so they start pushing people away, not because they don't want love, but because they fear it will only bring them pain.

But even in this darkness, there is hope. Healing is not easy, but it is possible. Sometimes, we meet people who see through our walls, who are patient enough to stay, and who teach us that we are worthy of love despite our past.

Parents love watching their kids grow up as they wish to cherish their childhood and youth. They feel proud watching their children turn into responsible adults, when they start working, when they start a family, whereas we hate to see our parents getting old. We cannot bear to see them getting weak, every day, because a part of us knows that someday, sooner or later, they will leave us behind, and this thought, this fear, breaks our heart.

How great it would be if we all could understand the real meaning of life while we have time?

When I planned to write this book, the first thing on my mind was that I should write something that helps people, something that the readers might be able to relate to their lives or someone they know. I have penned down the common family situations that I have observed around me in most of the households.

No one asks the kid, who lives in fear, how they feel about their parents' arguing day and night, like it is some sort of war, and one of them must win. Well, it's time that we change this mindset and realize that whatever the elders do, especially the parents, it affects the children in ways we can't even imagine.

I chose to write about sensitive topics like family situation, childhood trauma, love and friendship, because we all go through these stages in our lives. If this book helps even a single person to change and understand how much family is important, how much your character and behaviour at home, at work, anywhere, affects people around you, I would believe that this was the best investment for me because it would mean that I was successful in fulfilling the purpose of this book.

The story is set in Edinburgh for no specific reason. I have always loved those enormous, ancient-looking buildings and the weather there; therefore, I decided to write the story imagining the cold, rainy weather and the beautiful streets with huge structures. The characters and places are imaginary, but the situations are real, observed with keenness, and we all must have experienced one of these situations in our lives. If you have never struggled to be seen, to be heard, and to be loved, then trust me, you are blessed.

To my readers, if you have ever felt unseen, unloved, or burdened by the weight of responsibilities and your past, just know that you are not alone. I hope this story brings you comfort, understanding, and perhaps even a little hope that love—the right kind of love by the right person—can heal even the deepest wounds.

With love,

Nida Ali